MW01078552

Building and Spreading Faith through the Heart of a Child:

God's Melting Pot

Mary (Sweet) Harris

ISBN 978-1-0980-8675-6 (paperback)
ISBN 978-1-6387-4416-0 (hardcover)
ISBN 978-1-0980-8676-3 (digital)

Christian Faith Publishing, Inc.
832 Park Avenue
Meadville, PA 16335
www.christianfaithpublishing.com

New International Version (NIV)

King James Version (KJV)

Printed in the United States of America

This little children's book is to my four wonderful grandchildren: Ethan, Ty, Nasia, and Nylah.

This little children's book, entitled *Building and Spreading Faith through the Heart of a Child: God's Melting Pot*, I pray that each of you will experience at least three things. Even though it is a great possibility through my praying, you will experience even more. Nevertheless, those three things could be the following:

- How a little girl put the power of prayer to work in her life.
- How the power of prayer can become infectious.
- Lastly, you could experience the meaning behind the title of this book.

One day, Ella saw her father and mother praying and asked them, "Why are you always praying?"

MAMA. I pray because this is my way of talking to God to thank Him for what He has done, what He is doing, and what He will do for all of us. I especially thank God every day for my beautiful little Ella. It is times like this that we must thank God more than ever before because I want the world to become a happier place for all of us to live in. I want Him to protect you, always.

ELLA. Daddy, I heard why Mama prays. Now, why do you pray? Do you pray for the same things as Mama does?

DADDY. I do pray for the same things, and I pray for other personal things as well.

ELLA. So if I want something, so instead of bothering you and Mama, I should bother God?

DADDY AND MAMA. Ella, God never sees it as a bother when you talk with Him. If it is important to you, it is important to Him. Oh, by the way, Ella, we do not see it as a bother when you want to talk to us. You must remember that.

ELLA. Okay, Daddy. Okay, Mama.

MAMA. Ella, if there is something that we cannot do, then I want you to pray to God about it.

ELLA. Like what?

MAMA. Let me see! If you ask your daddy and me to buy you something. *Wait*! Ella, do not go to God always asking. You can start by thanking Him for all these blessings that surround us.

ELLA. I know. If I want to go over to my friend's house, and you say no, then I can tell God to make you let me go?

DADDY AND MAMA. No! No! Ella, some things are not going to be granted by God nor us. God knows what is best, and He knows the time and the way He wants to answer. I do not want you to ever stop praying, okay?

ELLA. Okay, Daddy and Mama, I will not. I like God. He sounds like you and Daddy. I want to do what you and Daddy tell me, and I want to do what God tells me. Mama, you want to know something? I believe I am going to need God very soon. You just watch!

DADDY. Okay, Ella, go and play now.

Ella went out to play, and along came a few of her friends. After minutes had passed, Ella told her friends about praying. She began to give thanks, and her friends heard her.

ELLA'S FRIENDS. Ella, who are you thanking and why?

ELLA. I am thanking God for all my friends because we make up something like new colors added to the rainbow. Well, anyway, if I made a rainbow, it will be just like us.

ELLA'S FRIENDS. You are silly, Ella. Let me ask you another question. Do you think you can tell me about this God you keep thanking for no reason?

ELLA. My mama said I must thank Him all the time because she said He has done so much, He is doing so much, and He will do so much again.

ELLA'S FRIENDS. God must be *soooo* tired because you are wearing him out! Eeewweeeh. When my mama tells me to clean my room, I get tired, you know Ella, when I talk about it, I get tired, again.

ELLA. You are so lazy and a kid. God is not lazy nor is He a kid. He is strong like Daddy.

As time passed on, one of Ella's friends contracted a cold that came with a fever. His name was Ty. Ella heard of this. She gathered all her other friends, Nylah, Nasia, Justin, and Ethan, and ran down to his house, but his mama said he couldn't come out to play because he did not feel well.

ELLA. My mama said God does not get tired, and she said to pray. Ty is my friend, and I want him, no! We all want him to get unsick, so we can always complete our rainbow.

TY'S MAMA. What, Ella? Complete a rainbow?

ELLA. Yes, our rainbow!

TY'S MAMA. Okay, Ella.

ELLA. Well, Mrs. Aliy, we all make up the new color rainbow. The new color rainbow would be just like us if I had made it. All my friends make up God's new color rainbow.

TY'S MAMA. I see what you mean. That is quite interesting.

ELLA. Me and my friends want to pray to God for Ty. May I? Because my mama and daddy said God can do anything. So I would like to see it for myself. Oh, I almost forgot, my mama said sometimes God may not answer. But I am going to see because if God is anything like my daddy, then I know He does not want to see Ty sick. He wants to see him very unsick.

TY'S MAMA. Okay Ella, you can pray right here.

Ella began to pray, and she stopped and asked her friends to join in. They did.

ELLA. God, help our friend, Ty, to get unsick. We miss him, and we love him. We must play and talk and laugh and act silly. God, you know the things kids like us do. God, we must complete our rainbow. Thank you, God. Amen!

After Ella, Nylah, Nasia, Justin, and Ethan prayed. Sometime later, Ty recovered. Ella could complete her rainbow.

ELLA. Well, I guess it worked. Now I see for myself.

NYLAH, NASIA, JUSTIN, AND ETHAN. What worked? What are you talking about now, Ella?

ELLA. Praying, silly. I am going to pray from now on.

NYLAH, NASIA, JUSTIN, AND ETHAN. We are going to pray from now on too. We like this praying stuff.

ELLA. I am going home now. I am tired because I am a kid too. Praying can tire a kid out. I will see you all tomorrow. God's new color rainbow is complete again.

To My Readers

I hope every child and parent has enjoyed reading this little book that has been ordained by God and written by me, Mary Harris. I believe if our little children would take on a positive viewpoint as to how they want to be treated, then and only then they will pass these attributes on to others. Just think how wonderful it would be, and the legacy they will leave behind!

I thank all of you for taking out your precious time to share your thoughts after having read this little children's book. Please take notes, write down your thoughts, and share them with other children who may not have learned to pray at this time. Just think of the feeling of satisfaction that you will receive and how it will fill other children's little hearts with such gratification for generations to come.

Pass it on!

Children, remember always: No one is smarter than you are, they just know some things you have yet to learn.

Parents' Corner

God laid this concept for this book upon my heart approximately ten months ago. Of course, I was not obedient. After ten months had passed, God came to me again. Guess what? I jumped up and begin to write. Let me just say I am not a writer, but when God says something in the manner He said it to me, I suggest you had better obey.

I had no idea this would be befitting in such a time as this. I am speaking of the horrific death of the many blacks in these past few months along with the pandemic, an epidemic of pandemonium proportions.

This little children's book is a twist on an old favorite because this isn't anything new. God gave me the idea and the stamina to remind us as parents that it is still good in the world, no matter what we have experienced, what we are experiencing, or what we may experience.

As parents, we must teach our children the power of prayer. We need prayer more today than ever before. I do believe this is what is needed for families, especially our children, not only here in America, but globally as well. I wanted to convey to all that there is hope, and miracles still lie in the power of prayer.

There is something else. We as parents must teach our children to love one another and not hate. All of us must remember our children are being taught even when we are not speaking. It comes louder through our demeanor and what other illustrations are being projected.

I am certain we are aware our children are going to learn so much from the world around them; therefore, we need to get to them first so we can guide them in the direction of what is right and not what is so wrong. When these little children learn from the world, they will only learn those things that the world wants to teach them, and, in the way, they want to reach them (you all know what I am talking about). This way of teaching could be either good, bad, or indifferent. The only way we can be certain they receive the right information is what is being taught by us.

One thing I am sure of, those whose hearts are filled with discriminatory issues have not been taught or do not live by the principle of the Golden Rule. Old as I am, I was taught this when I was a little girl in school.

Through prayer, the urge to execute unacceptable behavior can and will be put to rest. Discriminatory practices have negative connotations that must be replaced with positive ones. The question that comes to my mind is, Do I want to put in the time it takes to accomplish this much-needed task? Another question that comes to mind is, Who do I dislike? Is it others, or is it myself?

Parents, Many of our actions come from another source—jealousy. I think about why jealousy exists, and why we allow it to turn into hate. Guess what? I took it to God for a sound and lasting answer. This is what God gave me: Jealousy is when there is something that one has, which we want, and hate comes when we cannot get it. Think about that for a minute!

There is always an opportunity that presents itself for us all to do better, and when we have an encounter with others and/or situations, we would like for them to see God's Spirit, exuding from us. This very well could be the way others will see The God that lives on the inside of us, not our adversary.

I pray that all of you will grab a hold of something if only one word from reading this book. You can take that one word and allow it to become the most powerful word in your life today. I pray that you, as parents, have enjoyed reading this little book as much as I have enjoyed writing it!

Now that you have read the book, would you do me a favor? Ask yourselves as I have asked myself, What is just one unfavorable habit you would like to change? Once you receive the answer, then repent of that habit. Why did I say one habit? I believe that will be the beginning of changing something that you have been doing for years. If, at any time, you find yourselves turning back to old unfavorable habits after repenting, then please make a *U*-turn!

Please, remember we are all humans; therefore, we are subject to slipping and sliding (sinning). There is no way we can live a perfect existence in an imperfect world. Repentance is turning away from those old unfavorable habits and turning to God's way of doing things.

Love is the word of today and forever. If we come together in a collaborative effort to change, guess what, we can! Let me ask you. Are you willing to make that change? Please do not allow unforgiveness to penetrate your heart because I would like to believe we all want God to forgive us.

Lastly, parents, remember listening is one of the major aspects of communicating. Please carve out some time to listen more. Thanks!

May God continue to shower every one of you with His many blessings always.

Much love and appreciation,

—Mary (Sweet) Harris

Father God, in the mighty name of Jesus, I pray that You will cover everyone who has read this book, and those who have not, with Your precious blood today and every day. Amen and amen!

Scriptures to Remember

Do to others as you would have them do to you.

—Luke 6:31 NIV

If you believe, you will receive whatever you ask for in Prayer.

—Matthew 21:22 NIV

We love because He first loved us.

—1 John 4:19 NIV

Do not let anyone look down on you because you are young, but set an example for the believers in speech, in conduct, in love, faith, and purity.

—1 Timothy 4:12 NIV

Be kind and compassionate to one another. Forgiving each other, just as in Christ God forgave you.

—Ephesians 4:32 NIV

I can do all this through Him who gives me strength.

—Philippians 4:13 KJV

About the Author

Mary (Sweet) Harris was born in a small town in the State of Mississippi called Bourbon. She attended Lincoln Attendance Center High School in a town called Leland, where she earned a high school diploma in 1969.

In 1970, Ms. Harris left her hometown for California where she attended Sawyer's Business and Consumnes River College.

In 1971–1976, she became a mother of three wonderful sons, Eric, Rahman, and Hassan. Since that time, Ms. Harris has become a grandmother of four fabulous grandchildren, Ethan, Ty, Nasia, and Nylah, to which she has dedicated this book in their honor.

During these past years, she has attended Ultimate Medical Academy where she earned an associate degree in medical billing and coding. She attended Purdue University Global, where she has earned a bachelor of science degree.

Ms. Harris felt she had more to offer so she decided to take her educational experiences a little further. Currently, she still attends Purdue University Global earning a master's degree in health care administration where she is maintaining a 4.0 GPA.

Going back to school has given her the motivation and self-confidence she needed to prove to herself she could accomplish her objectives. She knew if she persevered and lock the door on *never* and *can't*, she could remove all obstacles that stood in her path. Ms. Harris has learned if she does not remove those obstacles, she could and would make them her steppingstones.

Ms. Harris prays her accomplishments will motivate others to join the rank of the seventy and seventy-plus years better to accomplish their objectives as well.